T.L. PRICE

REALM
OF THE
EXILED

REALM OF THE EXILED

EXILED ELEMENTALS SERIES

PREQUEL NOVELETTE

T. L. PRICE

CONTENTS

Also by T. L. Price   ix
Epigraph   xvii

Prologue   1
Chapter 1   3
Chapter 2   14
Chapter 3   23
Chapter 4   32
Chapter 5   38
Chapter 6   46

The story continues...   55
Exiled No More (Exiled Elementals) Book One   57
Acknowledgments   59
About the Author   61

ALSO BY T. L. PRICE

Exiled Elementals Series

Realm of the Exiled (Prequel Novelette)

Exiled No More (Book 1)

Enviro-Scapes (Book 2)

Ruins Awakened (Book 3)

EXCLUSIVE CONTENT

SEE ALL T. L. PRICE'S BOOKS, A PRONUNCIATION KEY, AND MORE ON HER WEBSITE AT:

https://www.TLPriceBooks.com

Newsletter Perks: Free book excerpts, character backstory, and book club questions when you sign up for my newsletter on my website. You also get updates on the release of future books, fun giveaways, and exclusive content. Get autographed copies of books, fantasy book boxes, fantasy maps, and book merchandise on my website.

THE MAP of TRACEA PANGEA
N
RUSSIA
EUROPE
GRECIAN ISLANDS
ICELAND
NORTH AMERICA
DRYLANDS
ARCTIC OCEAN WEST
SOUTH AMERICA
AMAZON
DEAD SOUTH OCEAN
THE GREAT DIVIDE
NORTH AFRICA
SOUTH AFRICA
MYSTIC OCEAN EAST
REALM of the EXILED
ARABIA
AUSTRALIA
PARADISE MESSEZHU
ANTARCTICA

N
NW NE
W E
SW SE
S
EUROPE
RUSSIA
ASIA
GRECIAN ISLANDS
VOLCANIC SEA
ICELANDS
NORTH AMERICA
DRYLANDS
TRAVALTA ISLAND
MYSTIC WEST OCEAN
AMAZON
SOUTH AMERICA
DEAD SOULS OCEAN
THE GREAT
CHILE

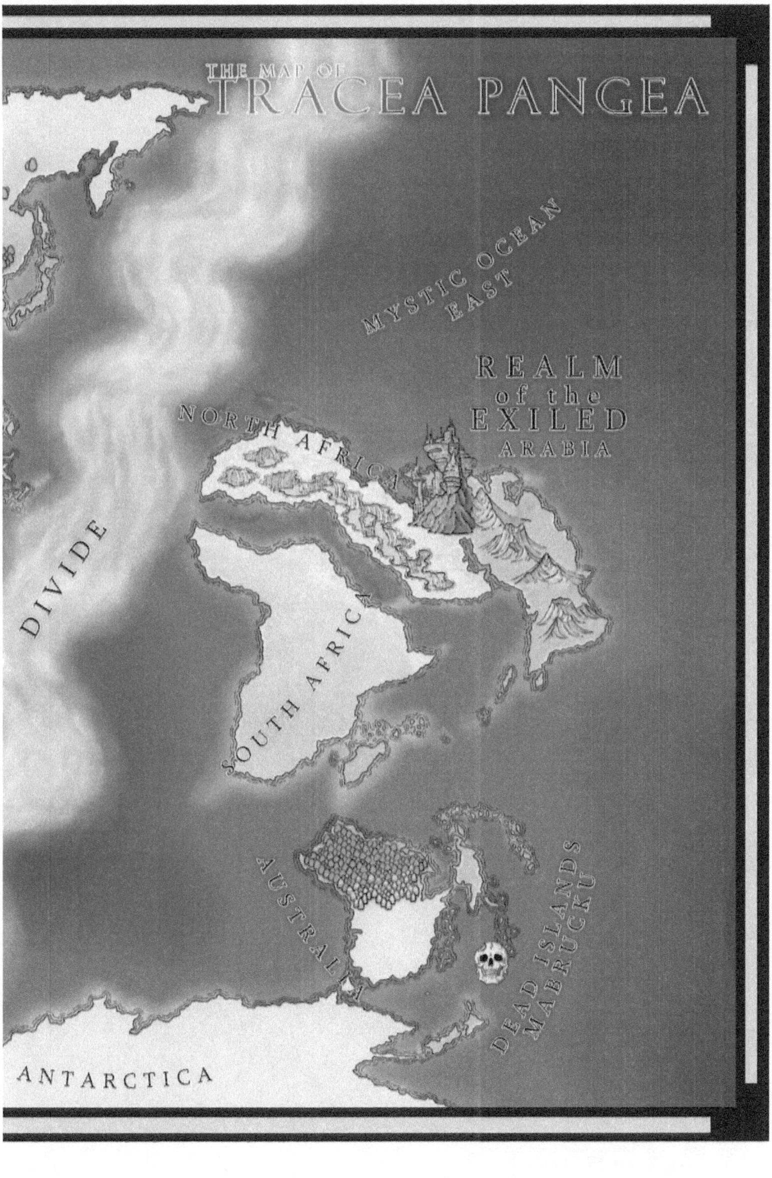

THE MAP OF
TRACEA PANGEA
MYSTIC OCEAN EAST
REALM
of the
EXILED
ARABIA
NORTH AFRICA
DIVIDE
SOUTH AFRICA
AUSTRALIA
DEAD ISLANDS
MABRUCKU
ANTARCTICA

EPIGRAPH

When desire and responsibilities collide, love is judged by those who undervalue your needs and those who know you need protection from what you crave.

T. L. Price

*When the Fall Harvest Festival Occurs on a
Full Moon,
Danger, Love, and Fate Become One.*

The exiled elementals will let nothing stop them from their celebration.

The Menu: *Danger, Tricks, and Treats.*

Yet, those living in the civilized world will not fare any better.

The Menu: *Deception, Threats, and Fine Dining.*

Two worlds will collide as they celebrate the fall harvest festival. Will the destiny of one decide the fate of the other?

CHAPTER 1

Nhari laughed as her exotic elemental tattoos roamed freely along her arms, casting beautiful glyphs circling her fingertips. She marveled as the bright green glyphs grew stronger and stronger as she cast them out into the trees. Within minutes, pomegranates blossomed on the trees.

"Who wants pomegranate tarts?" she called out to the anxious children, stunned at her elemental power. Nhari was the rarest of the elemental children. She could grow anything with her elemental power over plants. At just seventeen-years-old, her elemental powers were becoming one of the strongest among the elemental teens. Everyone clapped and cheered.

But Tiago had a show of his own. He stepped forward, muscles glistening beneath his ripped shirt, and bowed to the kids. Everyone waited to see his performance. Nhari and Kasha rolled their eyes, but they, too, wanted to see what he had in store for them.

His beautiful azure eyes lit with energy. Molten brown

elemental tattoos with striking patterns spiraled from his fingertips and blazed through the air into the trees. A few kids jumped out of the way as the glyphs arced through the air with such force they shook the ground and trees. Suddenly, the pomegranates fell, but they didn't hit the ground. Tiago was in rare form today. His magical powers held each pomegranate at eye level as the kids snatched them and carefully placed them in the waiting buckets to take back to their haven.

"Bravo, Tiago!" Kasha clapped as everyone joined in. Tiago's smile was like no other. He was the oldest of the group, now nineteen-years-old. He was growing into his taller height, adding more muscles every day. It was all set against a backdrop of devilish humor he could turn on with charm. He was breathtakingly handsome and clearly knew it. He grabbed his own bag of pomegranates.

"Where are you taking those tonight, Tiago?" Kasha quipped as she snatched the bag from his hands.

"None of your business!" he shouted as he tried to grab them back. But Kasha's elemental speed was unmatched. Each time he attempted to grab her, she moved like lightning out of his reach. Red elemental tattoos shimmered along her body in a unique hieroglyphic pattern, moving faster and faster. Kasha could set the world on fire with her powers and her beauty.

But Tiago was smart. He anticipated her next move, pulling the ground up around Kasha and blocking her path. She was stuck with nowhere to go as he grabbed the bag from her hands and pulled her long hair, eliciting quite a few choice words and laughter.

"He's taking them to his women in the Braven," Nhari playfully shouted.

Yes, Tiago knew how to woo the women prisoners, giving them gifts in exchange for intel and other things he didn't discuss with Nhari and Kasha. They knew Tiago did business with a tough crowd, but that didn't keep them from constantly asking him about his affairs.

As they walked back in separate groups, they looked over their shoulders to ensure they weren't followed. The elemental children were uncared for and unseen in the realm of the exiled, the notorious prison territory for the worst prisoners on Earth. The so-called civilized world cast prisoners to their doom, inoculating them from conceiving children. Yet, years later, numerous kids roamed the realm, abandoned by their parents. All but Nhari were born in the realm. It was the only world they knew. But Nhari knew more existed in the world, just out of their reach. But that world was now out of Nhari's reach, too.

She was exiled two years ago.

Nhari was no longer the royal brat of the ruling Guardian Clan. She was a shunned prisoner, always looking over her shoulder. Despite the harsh realities of being exiled, Nhari was happy to be free of her life with her wicked stepmother and late father. She had a new family now, and she had power. A power she was learning to use each day.

"Nhari, tell us about the fall harvest festival in the civilized world." The kids begged to hear stories about what existed outside the realm of the exiled.

"I have a surprise for everyone. We will throw our own fall harvest festival right here in the lava caverns. And I will make the best desserts you've ever tasted!" Nhari announced.

"We will hold it in three days when the moon is full. We will wear costumes, make crafts, and sing and dance. It will be the best festival ever!" Nhari beamed with delight. The kids were excited as they ran along the cavern, gathering the other children to hear the details of their festival.

"Tiago, you are the master of disguises. You're in charge of helping the kids find materials for their costumes. Adul oversees crafts, Kasha oversees music, and I'll come up with the menu." Nhari loved giving orders, as Tiago, Kasha, and Adul gave her fake salutes. They laughed and continued planning their first-ever festival.

"In the civilized world, all the ruling Guardian Clans celebrate the fall harvest festival, which is a celebration of life and fellowship." Nhari looked at everyone as they beckoned her to continue. She loved making everyone wait on her every word and smiled as one of the kids threw up his hands for her to hurry with her story.

"People of all ages wore elaborate costumes. The kids went door-to-door for treats while the adults went for *drinks and exotic pastries*. Oh, yummy!" Nhari picked up one of the pomegranates and twirled it in her hand. "There were lavish parties with balloons, lights, and dancing." Everyone clapped and began murmuring about their festival.

Nhari's eyes shone with pride for the excitement she created for the exiled elemental children—her new family. Nhari always knew she had special abilities, but it wasn't until she was exiled that she learned she was an elemental. In the realm of the exiled, as she went through puberty, her elemental tattoos blossomed, and her powers began to reveal themselves. She discovered the other elemental teenagers living in the realm, and together, they began training to use their hidden powers.

All the elemental children had exotic tattoos that appeared when they used their various powers. While Nhari's green elemental tattoos revealed her rare powers over plant life, Tiago's powers were quite different. Tiago's molten chocolate tattoos were powerful, allowing him to move the ground and other matter, including breaking and reshaping objects. Kasha's red elemental tattoos created fire, and her skin didn't burn. Their powers also gave them speed and strength, and some had special healing abilities. However, they were not invincible, as their harsh life made clear over and over.

That night, Tiago, Kasha, and Nhari headed out of their haven to the more dangerous terrain in the realm of the exiled. Tiago breathed in the night air. He enjoyed the feeling of being outdoors despite their proximity to the acidic oceans surrounding almost all sides of the realm. The realm was formerly known as the Middle East before it broke away from the continent many years ago. Though the realm still bordered North Africa, the realm couldn't be reached from that side due to an active volcanic ridge. Earth's entire geography changed over time due to cataclysmic changes in its tectonic plates and atmosphere during the Tracea Pangea. No one knew the cause, but they all lived in a dangerous world where the environment was just as deadly as the people fighting to survive.

"We need to stay low and quiet through this section," Tiago cautioned as they entered the mountainous caverns where many prisoners resided.

Though the realm of the exiled was a prison territory, it didn't have cells. Instead, the prisoners were bound to live as best they could in the harsh terrain with no way out. Prisoners had to make their own materials and grow their own food. Fortunately, many criminals were also skilled artisans exiled by the ruling Guardian Clans. The prisoners built homes, weapons, and many other tools that made life bearable. But tonight, the smell of death was in the air as Tiago, Kasha, and Nhari went about their business. Millions of prisoners were exiled to the realm, forced to live under the brutal control of the demigods who resided in the towering Overlord's fortress.

"Remember the rules, ladies. Stay out of sight and out of mind. Keep to the crowds and blend in. And try not to get caught stealing!" Tiago gave them a pointed stare as he ventured off with his pomegranate gifts.

"We make no promises," Kasha yelled back. She grabbed Nhari's hand as they ran into the Braven Quadrant using a different entrance than Tiago. The Braven was a dangerous trading post, offering almost everything the prisoners needed, including entertainment. The sprawling post stretched for miles with many mountainous chambers filled with tents, stalls, and structures. Old technology met new technology—sometimes side by side, making the Braven an eclectic mixture.

Nhari rummaged through her backpack. "Okay. I have one bag full of goods to barter and one bag to fill with whatever loot we can lift." She looked around. "I think we should be able to get what we need quickly, and then it's party time!" She gave Kasha a high five.

"A few of our alliances are already at their merchant tables. Let's see them last. We might be able to lift some supplies we can then sell to the merchants for a profit," said Kasha, surveying the area and exits. "I'll make a quick round of the place and return quickly." Kasha's elemental speed always came in handy when surveying the Braven for goods they could barter and goods they could steal. She was back in record time.

The girls were up to their usual mischief, seeking out the

finer things in life they could steal. There was one thing Nhari learned on her first day in the exiled realm. If you wanted something, you had to take it. There were no freebies here. Most died on arrival or went insane. But not Nhari...she was a survivor. And after meeting the wonderful elemental children, she was now a protector.

Nhari and Kasha saw Tiago laughing with a young woman as two more women stood nearby, trying to catch his attention.

"Look at Tiago working his mojo on those women! They are falling all over him." Kasha threw a lewd gesture Tiago's way, which he refused to acknowledge. Nhari threw one too, and they could see he was trying his best not to laugh.

"Did Tiago give you his normal lecture?" Using her best impersonation of Tiago's South African accent, Nhari continued, "Kasha, keep your distance from the dangerous men, and don't drink anything alcoholic."

Kasha laughed at Nhari's poor impersonation of Tiago. "He's always worried about us. We know how to protect each other's backs. I think he's just worried we will do whatever he's doing almost every night!" Kasha laughed again before continuing. "He's been more secretive than ever these last few days. I think he's into something that's more dangerous than usual."

"Well, that dress you have on is more dangerous than usual! Girl, it's cut so low you can't bend over in it!" Nhari laughed as Kasha bent over to touch her toes, only to reveal she wore a pair of stylish chain mail shorts underneath.

"If anyone tries to look under this dress tonight, they'll be sadly disappointed." Kasha winked.

"I love those shorts! You have to promise to make me a pair." Nhari marveled at the design. Kasha was quite handy at making fashionable clothing from chain mail mesh, a unique metal material that Kasha could melt down into mesh using her elemental power over fire.

"Yes, I'll make a pair for you. I'm sure you want me to add some of your fashionable belts and buckles to the ensemble, which seems to be your preferred style these days." Kasha looked at Nhari's current dress, which had elaborately braided belts dangling around the middle in pretty colors.

"I've always loved accessories, especially for my hair," Nhari commented.

"I love your hair, Nhari. Most people would kill for that reddish-brown color with those long thick curls. Your hair is down to your waist!"

"It's so hard to maintain, though. I wish I had met my birth mother to see how she cared for her hair. My dad's hair was black, so I know I inherited my hair, light bronze skin tone, and green eyes from her. My stepmother hated my guts since I reminded her of my mother, my father's mistress." Nhari twirled her curls, longing to know the mother she had never met.

"I look a lot like my mom too, though she abandoned me so long ago that I rarely think about how she looked. We both have a deep brown skin tone, slanted black eyes with hues of red and orange, high cheekbones, and long unruly hair."

"Have you ever considered going back to the fringes of the realm to look for your mother?"

"Hell no! She left me." Kasha continued, "besides, the fringes are so dangerous I wouldn't last one day living there now. We always had to run and hide. If you think living in the inner areas of the realm of the exiled is harsh, wait until you see how the prisoners live on the fringes of the realm."

"I was raised in Washington, D.C., but we traveled and lived in many places. My ability to quickly learn languages has been beneficial given the prisoners are from around the world. In fact, let's go put my linguistic skills to use as we barter for what we need." Nhari looked around devilishly. "Afterward, we can head to the best parties happening tonight."

The girls bumped their hips and then moved off into the deeper parts of the Braven. They looked back once but didn't see Tiago anywhere.

Nhari and Kasha had a very effective system to get what they wanted. Kasha would entice the merchants to look her way, while Nhari would walk past and steal whatever they wanted. Most of what they stole were things the younger exiled children needed to survive the upcoming winter storms, but tonight they were looking for craft items and party supplies for their fall harvest festival. After gathering their supplies, they sent them back to their haven with a rambunctious group of preteens.

"Hurry back to our haven. You know Tiago doesn't want any of you here in the Braven after midnight," Kasha yelled to the elemental preteens as they reluctantly left. The preteens were just as scared of Kasha as they were of Tiago. They both had a way of giving instructions that made you fear not following orders. Nhari laughed as the young preteens dashed back to their home.

Nhari and Kasha chatted as they moved between various merchant stalls, tents, and vendor establishments to find the best clubs the Braven had to offer. The nightlife was vivid as prisoners dashed here and there. They could hear the techno music and knew they were getting close to the best clubs.

"I'll tell your future for one of those silver bangles on

your wrist, young lady," a tarot card reader said to Kasha as she moved past. For some reason, Kasha felt compelled to take the offer.

"Sure, what do I have to lose? The night is still young," Kasha replied as she grabbed Nhari's hand and led them into the fortune teller's tent.

"Kasha, are you serious? This is a scam. Let's go!" Nhari exclaimed, feeling a bad vibe about the place. The old woman was missing several teeth, and the place reeked of goat blood and something else Nhari didn't even want to know about.

"I can tell your fortune too, young one. Sit down, and I'll give you a two-for-one deal." The woman smiled and winked her eye. Out of nowhere, a black cat jumped over Nhari's shoulder, landing on a table. It began hissing loudly at Nhari.

"I'm not interested. I'll wait outside," Nhari exclaimed, as she left the tarot card tent. Kasha stayed inside, curious to hear about her future.

The old woman directed Kasha to sit on cushions on the floor around a small table. The woman lit incense and grabbed a bag of bones from her pocket.

"That's odd," the old woman said almost to herself as she saw the smoke from the incense had turned a blood-red color. The cat jumped from the table and hid under a nearby chair.

"Was the incense supposed to change colors like that?" Kasha asked with rising unease, but the old woman didn't respond.

The fortune teller looked scared, hands trembling as she stared at Kasha. Finally, the woman gathered her nerves and read the first tarot card, which said Kasha had great power. Then the woman tossed a bag of bones onto the table. Gasping, the fortune teller jumped up from her cushion. Kasha jumped up too.

"Get out! You must leave now," the woman shrieked. "Something is coming for you!"

"What's coming for me? What are you talking about?" Kasha quickly cried, but the woman pushed her toward the tent door.

"Hey, do you want the silver bangle? Tell me my fortune!" Kasha replied, but the woman closed the tent door and locked it without another word.

"What the hell was that?" Nhari blurted, seeing how upset Kasha was at the encounter.

"I have no idea! She didn't even want the silver bangle."

"I told you it's some type of scam. The old woman is probably trying to scare you during the Halloween season. Let's go!" Nhari replied, smiling to cheer Kasha up. Kasha nodded; she wouldn't let the fortune teller get to her.

It was time for Nhari and Kasha to dance the night away. They entered a techno lounge and began dancing to the drummer's dangerous beat. The beat was intoxicating, driving the crowd wild. The girls fit right in, dancing and having a great time.

Later that night, Tiago looked in on the girls and saw them dancing and having fun. They were gorgeous and had dance moves most envied. He was tempted to join them on the dance floor, but he didn't have time. He was on an important reconnaissance mission. Seeing the girls were okay, Tiago left to find the weapons dealers he heard were bartering something dangerous.

CHAPTER 2

"Jacob, if the thief is in the Braven, we will catch him. This thief has exceptional talents to have lifted a weapon from an A-Lord. The A-Lord didn't notice his missing weapon until he got back to the Overlord's fortress, and as you can imagine, he is eager to get it back." Vigot looked at Jacob and the rest of his team.

"Trust me, Vigot. The thief will wish he had stolen a weapon from a prisoner instead of from an A-Lord. We don't need anyone brazen enough to steal from our military forces." Jacob cracked his knuckles as his luminescent eyes blazed with evil intent.

Vigot had faith that Jacob would find the thief. Jacob Gadot was a demigod with considerable power with a body built for battle. His metallic uniform showed the highest rank among the A-Lords. The A-Lords were the demigod's battle marines. Jacob was also part of the twilight legion, a rare group of demigods who carried twilight swords that could melt a person on contact. Vigot continued telling Jacob all he knew of the theft.

"The A-Lord recalls the description of a prisoner who bumped into him. No other prisoner had physical contact with the A-Lord, so that person must be the one who lifted the weapon." He described the thief to Jacob.

Vigot raised his brow, knowing Jacob wasn't going to like the next part. "And Jacob, when you find the thief, leave him to the A-Lord for punishment."

Jacob smiled a wicked grin. "I'll leave whatever is left of the prisoner!"

Vigot, Jacob, and the A-Lords branched out looking for the thief and anyone who helped him. The A-Lords were stationed on Earth to guard the Overlord's fortress and all it held. They also kept the prisoners in line, though today was a clear example of what could happen when a prisoner got out of control. Each A-Lord could take out a dozen prisoners single-handedly, using mind control and otherworldly weapons like the one the thief stole. The demigods had to retrieve the weapon before it was used against them.

Jacob watched Vigot move off down a corridor flanked by his twin demi-beasts. Vigot was the Overlord's son, and now the demigod in charge of the realm of the exiled. Jacob was second in command. Vigot was the only demigod on Earth bestowed with demi-beasts. They were a ferocious species bred with the male offspring of the Overlord, the leader of the demigods. They were telepathically linked to Vigot. No one wanted to be caught between their massive jaws. Each demi-beast was over ten feet long, muscular, and armed with razor-sharp claws.

There was a lot that Jacob admired about Vigot. He and Vigot shared a long friendship and fought together in many battles, despite their youth. Vigot and the Overlord were legendary among the demigods. But Jacob's family was also legendary. The Gadot family quickly rose through the demigod ranks for their bravery and intelligence. They were the most formidable allies to the Overlord's kingdoms in various sectors of the universe that the Overlord controlled.

After searching for nearly an hour, Jacob was no closer to finding the thief. Thousands of prisoners lurked in shadows while others did business of every kind in the many establishments in the Braven. Every prisoner that Jacob encountered quickly moved out of his way. Despite serving in the realm of the exiled for only six months, Jacob's reputation for brutality was already well-known to the prisoners. But Jacob had a sixth sense that told him he was on the path to an incredible discovery. Something primal was calling to him as he opened the techno door and entered the dance floor.

Kasha's favorite song roared on the DJ's speakers taking her to a level of energy she rarely felt. She could let her powers flow in the club, her red elemental tattoos masked beneath the roving lights of the club's lighting system. She was practically on fire in plain view, but no one could see the elemental in their midst.

Nhari left Kasha to her music as she ventured outside for air. Nhari was famished and wanted to sample some of the sweet delicacies sold along the Braven's merchant stalls. Despite the late hour, already past 1:00 a.m., merchants were everywhere selling their goods. The sights and sounds seemed to call Nhari as she ventured further down the dark passageways.

Back in the club, Kasha's moment of excitement was over as the DJ switched to a slow, sultry mix. She felt eyes on her instantly but didn't see anyone looking her way as she left the dance floor. She was used to the attention, a raving beauty like her mother. They could look, but they better not touch. Kasha sat at the bar, opting for a cool glass of water to help quench the fire still simmering below the surface.

Jacob's gaze had been on the center of the dance floor. He had never seen a human female like Kasha before. She was brimming with energy that shouldn't have been possible. Humans were considered a fragile and volatile species and rarely worth a demigod's sexual interests. Yet, there was something about her that was off. Jacob couldn't put his finger on it, but it was clear she called for close inspection.

Jacob's momentary distraction was enough to alert everyone inside that a demigod had entered the club. And not just any demigod, but Jacob Gadot, the deadly second in command. The prisoners quickly gathered their things and left by the exits furthest away from where he stood.

And then Jacob saw him. The thief that they were looking for. The thief took off down the corridor, knocking over prisoners as he ran. Jacob disappeared and reappeared at the thief's side in a flash. With one hand, Jacob grabbed the thief by his neck, raising him to eye level. The man struggled to break Jacob's hold. Three more prisoners with the thief tried to attack Jacob from the rear. They were brought down swiftly by the A-Lord, who had his weapon stolen. The A-Lord was out for blood and ready to match Jacob's savagery.

"He's all yours." Jacob threw the thief to the A-Lord. Then Jacob looked at the three prisoners who tried to attack him from the rear. His anger flared, an edge to his tone. "Well, today's not your lucky day!"

Jacob tortured each man as their screams echoed through the Braven corridors. He loved setting an example of prisoners to send a message that the demigods would not tolerate disobedience. But deep down, it satisfied Jacob's evil thirst for power over others.

Jacob then retrieved the stolen weapon, handing it back to the A-Lord. The A-Lord turned to the thief, who was still trying to catch his breath on the ground. The A-Lord pointed the weapon at the prisoner and vaporized him. There was nothing left but ash and a stench in the air of burnt flesh and blood.

Hiding nearby, Tiago marveled at the weapon, committing it to memory. One of his elemental gifts was the ability to replicate any technology he saw. He couldn't replicate the weapon without seeing its inner workings, but he could fashion something close if he found suitable materials. Prisoners sounded the alarm that the A-Lords were on the hunt. The A-Lords knew the thief must have had help and planned to roundup anyone who worked with him. It was time for Tiago to find the girls and take them home. They didn't want to get caught in the fighting.

As Jacob reentered the techno club, it was emptied of its patrons. Even the DJ was gone. The girl was gone with her strange energy. Jacob never saw her face, but he was sure he would recognize her somehow if he encountered her again. This required research. Jacob's father had sent him to Earth to uncover secrets about humans that demigods had buried long ago. He was sure his father didn't tell the Overlord about this mission for reasons that Jacob didn't understand. But there was one thing that Jacob knew for sure. Jacob was fixated on the girl and had to figure out what she was.

As soon as Nhari heard the prisoners screaming, she headed in the opposite direction. She knew Kasha could take care of herself. The elemental children knew two things: run when they heard screaming and never look back.

Nhari ran down a corridor with a large group of prisoners. Suddenly, the twin demi-beasts turned down the corridor she had just entered. Prisoners stopped in their tracks, trampling each other to turn around and go the other way. Nhari was pushed into the wall and lost her footing. The prisoners stepped on her, and some fell on her in the chaos. Nhari screamed in agony as she rolled into a ball to protect herself as the prisoners trampled her. Her elemental speed and agility got her back on her feet, but it was too late. Hundreds of prisoners fell over her, everyone struggling to get away from the demi-beasts.

As Nhari again tried to stand, the demi-beasts tore through the crowd, throwing people off her. They flanked Nhari's side as the crowd continued their stampede past them. The demi-beasts seemed to form a barrier between her and the group of frightened prisoners running to escape whatever havoc the A-Lords had planned.

Nhari was perplexed. *Why are the twin demi-beasts protecting me? I saved one of the demi-beasts months ago when it fell into a deep chasm. Does the demi-beast remember me?*

The second demi-beast walked on, but the one Nhari saved seemed to stare at her a moment longer. Its eyes were very intelligent. Without thinking, Nhari patted its fur and smiled. She giggled when the demi-beast seemed to smile back at her. She looked around to see if anyone saw her actually touching a freakin demi-beasts. But no one was in the corridor who was still alive.

After a few minutes, the demi-beast left her side, moving off to the shadows at the end of the hall. And for a second, Nhari thought she saw Vigot in the shadows. One blink of the eye and he was gone. Was it her imagination? She wasn't sure. But it was time to get the heck out of the Braven.

She met Tiago and Kasha at their rendezvous site. They hugged, grateful they made it safely out of the Braven. Tiago told them about the vicious attack Jacob and the A-Lords made on the prisoners and the thief. He also described how the A-Lord used the strange weapon to vaporize the thief. It was a new weapon they had never seen before. And it was one they never wanted to see turned against them. Tiago knew the thief ran a large weapons organization and the A-Lords would be looking for anyone affiliated with the thief. Tiago took a long breath, thankful he had never worked with the thief.

"We have to stay far away from the demigods. Even with our meager elemental powers that we're still learning how to use, we are no match against them," Tiago reminded the girls as they quickly walked home. It was pitch black outside, but Tiago continued to look over his shoulder to ensure no one followed them to their hidden location.

"Ever since Vigot and Jacob took command of the realm of the exiled, they have been relentless in requiring obedience. I heard an A-Lord say that Vigot is our age-equivalent and the youngest demigod to have an important command post like this. I sure wish the Overlord had sent him somewhere else." Tiago shook his head at the dangers they faced every day.

"The ruling Guardian Clans have sent so many prisoners here lately that everyone is vying for turf from the overcrowding. We are stuck between dangerous demigods and evil prisoners." Kasha walked and told stories about recent skirmishes happening among the prisoners.

Nhari remained silent in her own thoughts. She didn't tell them about her strange encounter with the twin demi-beasts or Vigot.

"Nhari, are you listening to us?" Tiago frowned, noticing Nhari seemed distant.

Tiago looked at Nhari with worry in his eyes. "I know you've only been in exile with us for two years. But we all need to remember the demigods are strong and dangerous. Don't forget what they are, Nhari. No one knows why they are here on Earth, and we don't want them to pay attention to us. No one can know we have elemental powers."

Nhari nodded but remained distant.

Only the worse prisoners on Earth were exiled to the demigods' prison territory. The exiled prisoners were dangerous, cutthroat, and cunning. Thankfully, the elemental kids were good at staying below the radar. They could walk into places and leave with stolen goods without anyone seeing them. Everyone thought the kids were harmless and defenseless, so they mostly left them alone. But sometimes, things got out of hand, and the kids learned to fight back.

Kasha trained them to be brutal and efficient in their fighting. It was a kill-or-be-killed setting. And when all else failed, they knew how to run and hide. Their elemental powers were still in their infancy. Tiago, Kasha, and Nhari were the oldest and most skilled. But even they had no idea what they could do with their powers with no adult elementals to teach them.

That night, Nhari dreamed of Vigot. Vigot was the sexiest demigod she had ever seen. All the women in exile, including the demigoddesses stationed there, whispered about Vigot's gorgeous body and the power he exhibited.

Nhari imagined Vigot kissing her and warming her body with his luminescence–a light force that made him glow. His smile was captivating, and his eyes were mesmerizing. Vigot was a royal bad boy, wearing expensive demigod clothing with a regal air. She loved a well-dressed man of power. Yet, Vigot also had numerous body piercings and a stern look that made him a warrior to be feared. No one knew why the demigods were on Earth or why the Overlord sent his son to rule over it.

Nhari knew she was out of her mind to dream about the most dangerous demigod on Earth. She remembered Tiago's warning to stay away from the demigods, yet she couldn't get her mind off Vigot.

Why am I not afraid of him? Why do I crave his attention?

Three days later, excitement bristled in the air as the kids got ready to celebrate the fall harvest festival that night. Everyone was busy running around the cavern preparing. It was going to be a full moon, and the atmosphere was ripe for the festivities.

"Tiago still isn't back from his nightly escapades! That boy is going to get caught with someone's woman again if he's not careful. He should have learned from the last ass-kicking he received." Kasha shook her head as she furrowed her brows in worry.

Nhari was also concerned. "Where do you think he goes at night? I tried to follow him, but he caught me by the arm and forced me to turn around. He said it was too dangerous for a beauty like me to be out so late at night in certain parts of the realm. I didn't listen to him, of course! But I lost track of him within the first hour."

"Speaking of secrets, you seem to be distracted. You've been acting strange ever since the demigods punished the thief in the Braven," said Kasha.

Kasha was very perceptive. Nhari knew she had to tell Kasha the fantastic news.

"First, you must promise to not tell Tiago. He will *kill* me if he finds out!" This certainly got Kasha's attention, and she nodded in agreement.

"Well, remember I told you I saved one of the demi-beasts and mended its leg in the past? I guess Vigot feels some sort of debt to me. So, he wants to meet me after our festival tonight."

"Are you freakin crazy? You're meeting with Vigot—the vicious-ass demigod who holds us captive?" Kasha shrieked, eyes wide. Seeing Nhari wasn't deterred, Kasha grabbed her by the shoulders to make her listen.

"Nhari, that demigod is dangerous! Why would he want to meet you alone in the dark? With a freakin full moon?"

"It's not for what you think, Kasha. Demigods rarely engage with humans sexually; at least, that's what everyone keeps saying. I think he wants to talk to me about something or thank me for helping his demi-beast. All I know is that one of the demigoddesses delivered his message to me yesterday." Nhari smiled at the thought of seeing Vigot.

Kasha didn't look convinced, but Nhari continued trying.

"Kasha, I have to go! I can't just ignore a command by Vigot—the vicious-ass demigod who holds us captive!" Nhari burst into laughter. Kasha laughed, throwing her hands up in defeat.

"Well, I'm going to go too. I'm not letting you face that *dangerous demigod* without backup!"

"*Hell no!* I'm not going with a *chaperone!* I will look like a teenage idiot if you show up." Nhari put her hands on her hips. Kasha laughed even louder.

"You're seriously going to go and see him, no matter what

I say, aren't you?" Kasha shook her head in disbelief. "Well, I will keep my distance. I just want to make sure you're safe. I will return home if everything seems fine. I won't tell Tiago where you went."

Nhari hugged Kasha. "Okay. So, what do I wear on my first date with a gorgeous, sexy badass demigod?"

The girls went to work fashioning the sexiest demigoddess costume they could create for Nhari. Kasha gathered her most delicate silks and sheer ribbons, making a beautiful dress with a sequined low-cut V-neckline. The middle of the dress had cutout patterns that Kasha pulled together with belly chains made of crystals found in their cavern. Nhari added her signature thigh-high studded pink boots with three-inch spiked heels. Next, they had to do something with Nhari's overwhelming hair.

"You certainly have *big hair* and a lot of it!" Kasha laughed as she tried to untangle it. Nhari screeched that Kasha was being too rough with her hair, but she loved when someone else tried to tame her tresses.

"Ah, that is beautiful!" Nhari marveled at what Kasha was able to do with her hair. Kasha tied it back with ribbons made of the same fabric as Nhari's dress, leaving tendrils of long curls framing her face.

By midmorning, Tiago had returned with many costumes for the kids, lights, and even a DJ stand! Whatever deals Tiago brokered in dangerous parts of the realm were clearly successful.

That evening, Tiago, Kasha, Nhari and the elemental children had the best fall harvest festival in the world. The elemental children lived in a series of caverns hidden in the southern volcanic mountain range of the realm of the exiled. The beautiful flowing red and orange lava made their cavern attractive, adding to the harvest theme. Despite the flowing pools of lava, the cavern had shafts that cooled the area where the kids resided.

Their fall harvest festival included a costume fashion show, trick-or-treating, and a huge party. The elemental children, some as young as two years old, walked the makeshift runway showing off their costumes to the others. Some were dressed as shifters who could turn into wolves and lions, though they were just myths. Some were dressed as bioengineered humans with sophisticated weaponry that they could control with their minds. Other kids were dressed as merchants, pirates, and Amazonian warriors. But none dared dress like an A-Lord.

Everyone cheered and laughed as the kids showed off their costumes and acted out the roles of those they portrayed in little skits. Adul and other preteens were dressed as witches and ghosts and pulled everyone into a huddle. It was story time. They told scary stories about the rituals of the Amazonian elders exiled to the realm, who everyone believed practiced human sacrifices. They chased the kids around the cavern, tickling the youngsters when they caught them.

The kids then went to various stations around the cavern to get treats and Nhari's pomegranate tarts. The sugar must have gotten to them because they were loud and wild. Tiago had drinks for everyone, carefully setting aside the adult drinks for him alone. Nhari and Kasha giggled as they swore they would find his stash before the night was over.

They celebrated well into the night. It was the best fall harvest festival they could have created. They sang and danced, finally ending the night with the sign of Suncorea. Suncorea was magical energy that linked the elemental children together. Their festival was undoubtedly one of fellowship and love. Nhari, Kasha, and Tiago felt pride and joy that they had given the elemental kids a night they would always cherish. Despite the hardships of growing up in a prison territory without parents, the kids were full of love and hope.

Afterward, Nhari stole off into the night with Kasha close on her heels. Nhari went far off into the more dangerous terrain of the realm. The mountainous terrain was rocky as she traveled through the mountainsides, with steep drop-offs that looked like endless pits in the dark.

Along the way, Nhari got scared. She thought something was following her but didn't see anything. When she stopped and looked around, she saw shadows, creepy spiders, and other night crawlers. The night was full of eerie sounds, and her imagination was starting to get the best of her.

Finally, Nhari was so spooked that she almost turned back. But she saw a bright pair of eyes ahead as the demi-beast cautiously jumped down from the ridge above her. It motioned her to get on its back. As she reluctantly climbed on its back, it leaped off the cliff.

Nhari screamed, but they landed safely below. Vigot was standing there laughing, seeing the look on her face.

"That was really messed up! *I could have died!*" Nhari yelled at Vigot before realizing who she was actually yelling at. A smirk spread across his lips as he stared at her from a distance.

Nhari was pissed. Her long hair had come undone from the jump, and she was disheveled, trying to get off the back of the demi-beast. Vigot stood in silence, which only pissed her off more.

"Well, are you going to say something? Are you going to apologize for scaring me?" Nhari demanded with her hands on her hips.

In an instant, Vigot went from standing ten feet away to standing directly in front of her. Nhari found herself staring at the most enormous muscular chest she had ever seen on a man. At nearly seven feet tall, Vigot stared down at her with that same smirk. Nhari strained to look up at him, marveling at the piercings through his eyebrows and ears. She was totally captivated as he looked into her eyes, as his smirk grew wider.

Suddenly, without warning, Vigot grabbed her hair...and gently pulled it behind her ears.

"There. You look beautiful." Vigot's deep, husky voice melted her to the core.

His luminescent glow seemed to get brighter as Nhari's blush matched its brightness. Nhari knew she must have looked like a ripe tomato as she smiled from ear to ear.

"You are the most exotic beauty I have ever encountered, Nhari Evans!" Vigot licked his lips, letting his forked tongue with two piercings capture and hold her attention.

Vigot was dressed to impress. His eyes roamed over Nhari's beautiful dress, making it clear he liked what he saw.

But the moment was short-lived. Whatever Vigot had planned for Nhari, they weren't going to find out.

"*Get the hell away from her!*" Tiago shouted as he catapulted down from the ledge with a rope. Tiago drew his weapons and yelled for Nhari to move out of the way. Kasha climbed down the rope next, nearly out of breath, as she rushed to Nhari's side.

Vigot disappeared into thin air. But Tiago felt the air shift just as Vigot reappeared to his left, lifting Tiago from his feet and throwing him across the ground. Within seconds, the demi-beasts surrounded Tiago, using their massive paws to pin him down. Vigot disarmed Tiago and looked at him viciously.

"Vigot, please don't harm him! He's my friend," Nhari shouted.

Vigot ignored Nhari's pleas as he stood over Tiago and surveyed Tiago's weapons. Everyone noticed Vigot's luminescent glow had changed to a strange color that looked deadly. His strong hands with clawed fingernails crushed Tiago's metallic weapons with minimal effort, leaving dust he purposely shook into Tiago's face.

Tiago was livid at being held down, forced to look up at Vigot, practically defenseless. Tiago couldn't afford to use his elemental powers unless there was no other option. They had to keep their elemental powers a secret from everyone, especially the demigods. And they knew there was no way they could beat Vigot. Even combining their elemental powers, they were no match for a skilled battle-proven warrior who could use mind control and other demigod powers to crush them. They were at Vigot's mercy.

Vigot seemed to rein in his anger. He used his mind-link with the twin demi-beasts to command them to release Tiago. The demi-beasts growled and then let Tiago go. Tiago jumped up, fists balled at his sides, clearly still angered by the situation. But he didn't approach Vigot. Tiago was pissed, but he wasn't stupid.

Vigot turned with his demi-beasts, all three disappearing into the air. He reappeared at the top of the cliff and yelled down. "The winter storms are arriving early this year, Nhari.

I came to warn you to get ready. It's going to be a long and deadly winter."

And then he disappeared from the ridge.

No amount of apology would work on Tiago as Nhari followed him back to their lava cavern. They couldn't be sure that Vigot didn't follow them, so they took a long circuitous route back. It was a long, daunting walk.

"Nhari, I'm sorry I ruined your date. When I heard your scream, I thought Vigot had attacked you. And then I saw that Tiago had followed us. We came to rescue you," Kasha explained with sincerity.

"We shouldn't have had to rescue you! You shouldn't have been there in the first place!" Tiago glared at her. "*A date with a demigod?* How *stupid* are you, Nhari? Who *knows* what he was up to?" He yelled and cursed.

"I'm telling you, Tiago. He wasn't trying to harm me. I only screamed because the demi-beast jumped from the cliff. I didn't know what was happening," Nhari pleaded, but Tiago wasn't listening. Kasha also looked unconvinced that Vigot wasn't up to something dark and scary.

"He's a young demigod looking for fun. Despite his youth, he's still a warrior and one of the most powerful demigods on Earth. He's the Overlord's son!" His focus serious, Tiago clenched his jaw. "Do you know what kind of powers he must possess? What makes you think he wants something good from you?" Tiago yelled as he used his elemental powers to violently crush nearby rocks. His anger continued to boil.

"Calm down, Tiago! I think we can trust Vigot. He warned us that the winter storms are coming early. Why would he do that if he intends to harm me?"

Vigot's warning about the impending winter storms was

critical advance information. Like everywhere on Earth, the realm of the exiled went through seven seasons, with the winter season the worst. The snow froze everything on contact. Many prisoners lost limbs and their lives if caught unaware or without enough food stored to survive the winter months.

"Men will say anything to get what they want. Demigods are no different. How do you think I get intelligence and weapons from the women in the realm of the exiled? I tell them whatever they want to hear. I make them feel whatever they want!" Tiago shook his head. "Don't be naïve, Nhari. A demigod doesn't want anything good with a human female!"

Nhari blinked back tears, eventually tuning Tiago out as he continued to chastise her. She thought about Tiago's words and knew he had forgotten one thing.

I'm not just a human female. I'm an elemental.

CHAPTER 4

On that same day, the civilized world was preparing for their fall harvest festival. To most people, Angela and Krista looked like two women enjoying fine dining at an exclusive restaurant on Travalta Island in the civilized world. They were middle-aged, beautiful, and having fun. But for some, they steered clear of the most dangerous women to wield their power in the world. Angela Evans was a member of the ruling Guardian Clan that controlled all the governing functions in North and South America. Yet, her reach was far more significant.

Angela and her deceased husband created the bio-pill empire that allowed humans to traverse the Earth using jump portals that appeared after epic events in Earth's geological history. The portals allowed humans to jump from one location to another on Earth. But it came with a price—one that Angela set and controlled. Humans needed bio-pills to prevent their bodies from decaying through the jump portals. Bio-pills were very expensive. They were also rumored to cause an addiction, making those who could afford to pay its price use them more than needed.

The bio-pill empire wasn't the only thing that gave Angela power. No, those who competed with her knew her power resided in something else. Angela also ran a formidable bio-medical lab where extreme bioengineering of humans took place. Angela and her sons could do things that rivaled what people used to see on shows about superheroes. They were stronger and could live longer than most humans. Their bioengineering made Angela so fierce that it likely would take ten armed men to subdue her. Yet, it wasn't Angela that people feared most. It was her son, Micah, an armed assassin who purged the family line of any who opposed his mother.

But some clans wanted to stop Angela Evan's reign. Those powerful ruling Guardian Clan families rivaled Angela, and they were secretly allying together to remove her power around the world.

This only made the alliance between Angela Evan's and Krista Winters' families more vital. Krista was an esteemed scientist who cracked the code enabling humans to program jump portals to travel from one location to another. Krista charted all the known jump sites on Earth and used her technology to allow jump portal travel. While she was a scientist, she was also a ruthless power broker. Since Krista controlled the primary means that Guardian Clans around the world traveled, they had to bend to her will. And many lost their lives when they failed to fulfill the bargains they struck with Krista and her powerful and secretive family. Together, Angela and Krista could change the course of the world.

That afternoon, while the rest of the world was getting

ready to celebrate the fall harvest festival, the ruling Guardian Clans from every nation were meeting on Travalta Island. It was a great time to meet to celebrate their accomplishments and plan for the year ahead. The island was where the rich and famous partied, held conventions, and delved into all that the world offered, both good and bad. Anything could be bought and sold on Travalta Island, where business and entertainment never stopped. The island was formed many years ago off the coast of North America and was surrounded on almost all sides by the Volcanic Sea. It also held the largest arena ever built, where each nation brokered their treaties and competed for more power. The island was cloaked in mystery and superstition and governed by one family–the Armagenons.

"I open this meeting of the ruling Guardian Clans around the world. Everything discussed is governed by the ancient scrolls that dictate the rules of order." Arcadius Armagenon rose around the Armagenon Arena on a gliding podium. His voice was frightening, echoing around the room and through the holo-visions of those participating remotely. Arcadius continued his opening remarks.

"Long ago, wars raged among humans as they fought for scarce resources. Humans ultimately created four ruling Guardian Clans that governed large geographical regions. Please stand as I call your clan for acknowledgment."

Arcadius then called each of the four clans, as they rose with pride to be the elite governing forces of the world. He called the American Guardian Clan, the Euro-Russian Guardian Clan, the Afro-Australian Guardian Clan, and the Asian Guardian Clan. Each clan ruled their territory with an iron fist and fought viciously to gain more control over Earth's scarce resources.

Angela stood and spoke on behalf of the American

Guardian Clan. When Angela announced the price increase for bio-pills, the reaction was quick. The Euro-Russian Guardian Clan was the first to express their outrage. They threatened to pull their membership from the ruling Guardian Clan council and to cease all peaceful talks. But everyone knew they were bluffing. They needed the bio-pills to travel through the jump sites, given their territory was covered with so much ice that it was their primary source of travel. Angela smirked in their direction, knowing she had them where she wanted them.

The Asian Guardian Clan sat silently, but everyone knew they were probably hatching a plan. They were cunning and unpredictable, which made them deadly.

However, no one expected the retaliation that came swiftly from the Afro-Australian Guardian Clan, which was making its own power grab. That territory had some of the best food resources in the world, many of their lands fertile, and their oceans accessible for catching seafood. They simply stood and vowed to increase the price of all seafood to those who approved Angela's bio-pill price increase.

The meeting was chaotic as the clans shouted, threatened, and negotiated. In the end, the American Guardian Clan increased Angela's bio-pill price, and the Afro-Australian Guardian Clan increased their food prices. And so began the food wars.

Arcadius intercepted Krista and Angela as they left the council meeting.

"You are creating unnecessary battles with ruling Guardian Clans that we need in the future, Angela. There was no need to increase prices on bio-pills that are already too high."

"Arcadius, you worry too much! Things will settle down,

and the price will be absorbed into the system. My research is expensive, and the bio-pill manufacturing costs are ever-increasing." Angela smiled wickedly. "I'm not greedy if *that's* your concern! I'm merely trying to create a sustainable bio-pill supply chain to help the world," Angela dismissively stated.

Arcadius laughed, but the pitch was not humorous and full of mockery and disdain. "Angela, you may think the Afro-Australian Guardian Clan is weak and won't carry out their threats. But I can assure you that they are becoming very powerful as the world's oceans become more acidic and the lands less nutrient-rich. They are gathering more allies than you know."

Krista intervened, rolling her eyes. "Surely there is *enough* food to put on everyone's tables, Arcadius! A little price increase won't send people to their deaths."

"Speaking of deaths, Angela, your husband's untimely death has given you two votes at every ruling Guardian Clan council meeting. Combining your votes with Krista's votes gives you power that some are looking to take away. I've heard rumors that some are looking into a way to remove that second vote from you, Angela. Your husband *is dead*, after all!" Arcadius' mystical eyes darkened as he looked down on Angela. Arcadius walked away, leaving the women to think about his not-so-subtle warning.

Angela and Krista didn't like the prospect that Angela's second vote from her deceased husband could be taken away. It had long been council governing rule that if a clan leader was murdered, their vote would go to their surviving family. The law was in place to prevent people from making assassination attacks on ruling Guardian Clan members believing it would decrease their voting power.

Angela was visibly upset. She still missed her husband dearly. He had been dead now for a little over two years, a life stolen away by his murderous daughter.

"Arcadius is likely behind the coup to remove my second vote! How dare he suggest it might be possible!" Angela was livid, which was a bad thing. Krista could see the wheels turning in Angela's dangerous mind.

Krista was also concerned. "Arcadius is making his own power grab. He is already very powerful as the leader of the Trials of Guardianship. His ruling body determines which family heirs are placed on future ruling Guardian Clan councils worldwide. Arcadius is his own governing faction, reporting to no clan. What more does Arcadius want?" Krista looked at Angela for a response, but she had none. Both women were growing very concerned at Arcadius' actions.

"We cannot go up against Arcadius, Angela. He is too powerful. Regardless of what we think of him, his family has wielded great power for a century. We don't want to end on opposite sides of any battle with the Armagenon family." Krista was smart and calculating, and she would not make a reckless move against Arcadius.

"I agree. Even I don't want to take that old bastard on. You should go to him, Krista, and try to work out some agreement. He likes you, and he always has. I think he mentioned this to us because he already has something that he wants from us. Go to him to find out what he wants." Angela was still mad, but she knew they had to make a deal with Arcadius.

"I'll go to him, Angela. But what if the price is too high?" Neither woman wanted to think about that possibility. But Angela and Krista were warriors at heart. And they were a deadly force when they worked together.

CHAPTER 5

Krista's request for a meeting with Arcadius was summarily rejected. That wasn't a good sign. Krista and Angela knew Arcadius was up to something, their allies telling them that he was meeting behind closed doors with select ruling Guardian Clan families. No one knew which families were invited to the meetings, but everyone wanted an invite. They all knew it was dangerous to be left out of Arcadius' bargaining room.

It was a full moon, and the feeling of dread was everywhere. However, Angela and Krista weren't going to let Arcadius or the other clan families usurp their power. It was the night of the fall harvest festival, and they intended to enjoy it.

That night, partygoers everywhere enjoyed the fall harvest festival in the civilized world. Travalta Island was the best place to celebrate. Angela and Krista partied with their friends and family. They both wore elaborate costumes and entertained their families at one of the island's exclusive members only clubs. A huge assortment of foods from around the world, drinks, and entertainment beckoned everyone to enjoy.

However, at midnight, their party was interrupted. Arcadius' private armed guard approached Krista and Angela as they sat laughing with their group. Arcadius summoned both women to come to his home immediately on the far side of Travalta Island.

"How dare he *summon us!* Where was the courtesy invitation? Arcadius' grab for power is going too far, Krista. He must be dealt with!" Angela was outraged at being summoned as if she were not one of the most influential women in the world. "Arcadius is powerful, but his old ass will die one day! If he isn't careful, it will be sooner than he thinks!"

"Angela! Watch your threats! Arcadius wields unique powers that no one has ever challenged. He has spies and ears everywhere, and we cannot go up against him." Krista looked around to ensure no one had overheard Angela's threat.

"And what if he leaves us no choice, Krista? What then? We cannot let anyone usurp our power, or we will become weak and irrelevant," Angela defiantly replied.

"Let me negotiate with Arcadius when we enter the room. As you've said, he seems to favor me." Krista was a fierce negotiator. While she would put on a face of charm, she was a hyena that would steal your young for dinner.

Angela agreed it was best to let Krista handle the negotiations with Arcadius. They got into armored vehicles and went to his mansion, which was a towering set of buildings in the ultra-modern city on Travalta Island. The guards stayed at their side as they entered Arcadius' private chambers, locking the door behind them.

"I've had a vision. It shows the course of humanity is on the brink of a great war and possible extinction!" Arcadius rotated around the room on a flying podium with additional guards entering the room. He meant for Krista and Angela to stay until he was finished, and he intended to deliver his deadly message whether the two powerful women wanted to hear it or not.

Krista's powers hummed beneath the surface as soon as the guards placed their hands on their weapons. Angela powered up her artificial intelligence (AI), syncing it with her brain and the bioengineered weapons she wore under her costume. Angela was a powerful bioengineered human armed with the latest classified weapons. She aimed them at Arcadius.

Angela's act of defiance would be her undoing.

"Your AI will not work on me, Angela. Power down or feel my wrath!" Arcadius boomed through the air, though the sound was so close to Angela's ear that she flinched, believing he was standing behind her. Yet, he never left his podium in front of them.

"Enough of your games, Arcadius!" Krista shouted. "Why were we summoned? We are not here to fight. But when you meet us with an armed guard blocking our exits, we will fight until the bitter end." Krista forced her powers to stay beneath the surface, knowing she could not reveal her secret abilities to Arcadius or Angela.

Several minutes passed as the standoff ensued until Angela powered down. Arcadius' guards lowered their weapons.

"I've allowed you two to grow in power. And what have you given me in return?" Arcadius glared at them. "The Armagenon family stood against the demigods and other powerful beings when the Earth was torn apart, yet *you* seem to forget our role! Do you think I'm making a power grab? I already have the POWER! You are just too egotistical to realize it." Arcadius' voice was deadly and stern.

"Get to the point! I didn't come all this way for a lecture, Arcadius. Or to be threatened when I have not forsaken you." Angela screamed, her voice alerting everyone that she still commanded her AI with brutal precision to do great harm if pushed further.

"Please! You both must calm yourselves," Krista told Arcadius and Angela to try to calm the scene, though Krista's powers still secretly hummed beneath the surface. Lowering her voice to a soothing tone, Krista continued her negotiations.

"Arcadius, you didn't call us here if you didn't have a plan in mind. Tell us what you want so we can be done with all the posturing." Krista pointed to the guards with emphasis. "I share Angela's distaste for your threatening treatment of the two women who have *always* stood allied with you." Krista calmly pointed out.

Angela and Arcadius looked at each other for a moment and nodded a temporary truce. Arcadius glided down to the floor. Even on the ground, he towered over the two women, who did not shrink from his size.

"The Trials of Guardianship have always been the way that we test future heirs who will lead our people. My visions have shown me that these heirs will be up against a war that will determine the fate of humanity! As a result, I must make sure that only the strongest heirs survive the Trials of Guardianship." Arcadius shook his head as if fearing what was to come. He was a psychic of unparalleled abilities. Arcadius continued.

"It has come to my attention that you both have heirs who will compete in the Trials of Guardianship. *Your heirs* worry me!" Arcadius' evil smile hit its mark as he looked at Krista and Angela, as they realized the power Arcadius wielded over their children's lives.

"I have one more heir, my youngest son Thayden, who will enter the Trials of Guardianship. Thayden is no threat to you, Arcadius. He is a good and honorable person." Krista was walking on a thin rope. Her youngest son, Thayden, would compete in the upcoming Trials of Guardianship. Thayden's young life would be on the line every day...a life that Arcadius would fully control as the sole commander of the Trials of Guardianship. Krista's heart raced, trying to determine whether Arcadius had ill intentions toward her son.

The Trials of Guardianship was a ritualistic coming-of-age competition that all children of ruling Guardian Clans entered when they turned the age of twenty. Arcadius had sole power over the competition, which was deadly but vital in determining which heirs could take a seat on the ruling Guardian Clan councils in the future.

Arcadius looked at Krista ruefully. "I hear that Thayden is quite the mystery. I also hear he has a habit of disappearing on adventurous voyages. I do love solving a good mystery."

Krista wasn't going to take the bait. "I can assure you there is no mystery that requires solving where Thayden is concerned. He is a youth having fun, and nothing more." She didn't want anyone looking into Thayden's secret adventures. Hell, even she didn't want to know what her son was into.

Arcadius turned his evil eye towards Angela. Angela looked at Arcadius fiercely as she spoke of her own heirs.

"And I have two heirs, Micah and Arion, who will enter the Trials of Guardianship in the future. In fact, my son Micah will enter the same Trials of Guardianship competition as Krista's boy. Our sons will serve this world well." Angela glowed with pride.

"No, Angela! Your sons will serve YOU well. Everyone knows that your son, Micah, does your bidding. Does he have a mind of his own? You already wield two votes on the ruling Guardian Clan council and wreak havoc with it. The other families will do everything possible to keep you from getting another vote." Arcadius looked genuinely concerned as he walked around the room and knocked back a glass of brandy before pouring a second.

He offered Angela and Krista a cocktail, which they gladly accepted. They all needed a drink since the conversation turned into one threatening the lives of their heirs and the future of humanity. Angela was the first to speak after a long awkward pause.

"I know I have lots of enemies, Arcadius. But my heirs, Micah and Arion, *will serve well.* And if anyone, and I mean anyone, attempts to harm a hair on their heads, I will tear this world apart!"

Arcadius smiled like a viper. "You forget, Angela. The Evans family has *three heirs!* Nhari Evans, your stepdaughter, is also an heir to her father's legacy."

"My dearly departed husband HAD three heirs. The illegitimate heir, my husband's delinquent daughter, Nhari, is exiled. She was exiled as a child for her horrific crime." Angela smiled. "And I can assure you, she is already dead in the realm of the exiled. And even *if* she had somehow survived, she has forfeited her life and cannot return to the civilized world. Once exiled, you can *never* return. Nhari

Evans is the property of the Overlord now." Angela beamed with satisfaction.

Minutes passed as the three stood silent, each calculating their next response. Krista wondered why Arcadius was worried about her youngest son Thayden entering the Trials of Guardianship. Angela was also concerned about the safety of Micah and her younger son Arion. She was almost certain Nhari was long dead.

Finally, Arcadius nodded to the guards to unlock the doors and open them. He turned to Krista and Angela one last time.

"Make sure your heirs are ready for the battles to come. The world will depend on them *if* they survive their Trials of Guardianship! You are dismissed."

Krista and Angela quickly left the room, not looking back. While they were fearless women, they were all too happy to live another day and not battle with Arcadius. His chambers felt like death was waiting to eat away their very souls. The Armagenon family had strange powers that Krista and Angela didn't want turned against them. Travalta Island was a mysterious land mass that Arcadius controlled. Those locked inside his arena over the years were mysteriously found dead, and Angela and Krista didn't want to be among them. They rejoined their families at the fall harvest festival.

Arcadius pondered Angela's belief that Nhari had forfeited her right to compete in the Trials of Guardianship. It was a case of first impression because an heir had never been exiled. Arcadius had vital work to do. The ancient scrolls were the only rules that governed the Trials of Guardianship system set up so many years ago by his ancestors and the demigods. In fact, most of the ruling Guardian Clan families didn't know demigods existed.

Arcadius needed to consult the scrolls to find a rule to ensure all the heirs, including Nhari, would compete in the Trials of Guardianship when they turned twenty-years-old. He would ensure that only those who served *his* needs would leave the future Trials of Guardianship alive. If Nhari Evans grew as powerful as her birth mother, she would be a wild card in everything he saw in his visions of the future world. Arcadius had many secrets he didn't share with Krista, Angela, and the other ruling Guardian Clan families. Arcadius quickly gathered his things to research the scrolls.

CHAPTER 6

Back in the realm of the exiled on the night of the fall harvest festival, all was not well. Vigot was brimming with anger when he reentered the Overlord's fortress after his first date with Nhari.

The fortress was a magnificent structure built by the greatest demigod architects in the galaxy. Its honeycombed-shaped buildings scaled the highest mountain in the realm of the exiled, with floating terraces and balconies around its upper chambers. The walls were made of materials found on Earth and some from beyond, including rare crystals that made various upper rooms glow with energy. The Overlord's fortress housed the A-Lords and demigods stationed on Earth, and the Overlord when he visited. It also housed many other secrets. And in the center of the fortress stood a jump portal so powerful that people could jump from one side of Earth to the other in seconds.

Vigot's quarters were regal, with no expense spared to bring the finest furnishings and appointments the demigods had off-world. The floor, wall, and ceilings were made of beautiful crystals that powered everything in the room. He had technological systems that allowed him to see beyond Earth. Despite the beauty around him, Vigot's anger made him want to tear the place down. He thought about what had just happened.

How dare the one they called, Tiago, attack me! And why did Nhari bring him and Kasha along without telling me? Why did she come if she didn't trust me?

He wanted to tear Tiago limb from limb. Vigot only had honorable intentions for Nhari and didn't intend any harm to her. Yet, Vigot had to be honest with himself. Nhari had no way of knowing his true intentions. He was a demigod, after all. The very demigod who was forbidden from getting into the prisoners' affairs. He was supposed to rule over them. Vigot wasn't supposed to give them gifts and help them survive the brutal conditions on Earth that humans had all but destroyed with their greed. And he certainly wasn't supposed to take a female prisoner on a date.

Vigot threw his hands up in frustration. Nhari had gotten under his skin since the first time he caught a glimpse of her months ago. One of the twin demi-beasts had fallen into a dangerous precipice, breaking its hind leg. It landed on a ridge about to break that would have sent the beast falling further into the chasm until Nhari rescued it. She helped his demi-beast with gentle care, despite fearing for her life. The demi-beast could have eaten her whole. There was something strange about Nhari that drew Vigot to her. It was as if Nhari had an energy force around her that Vigot caught a glimpse for just a moment before she saw him. He couldn't get her out of his mind ever since.

Even her outburst made her unforgettable. Nhari dared to *yell* at a demigod. Vigot was totally turned on, whether he wanted to admit it or not. Nhari was a a stunning human female, yet there had to be more to her.

Caught in his thoughts, Vigot didn't feel his father in his mind until it was too late. The Overlord had telepathic abilities that defied logic. The Overlord could cast his mind out to the universe and ensnare the minds of his offspring. It was called the Ourani tether, an ancient technique that only those with the strongest minds could use. The Overlord didn't like what he saw in Vigot's mind and instantly appeared in person in Vigot's quarters.

The Overlord stood a few inches taller than his son, with muscles rippling beneath his armored uniform. The luminescent glow blazing around the Overlord was so fierce that most couldn't look directly at him, for it was almost like looking at the sun. But today, the Overlord's luminescent glow was dark and full of concern.

"My son, your mind is on a course that doesn't fit your true purpose here on Earth. Have you lost your way, Vigot?" The question was a dangerous one coming from the Overlord. Son or not, the Overlord would not tolerate Vigot veering from the course he had carefully laid so many years ago. The demigods were on Earth for important reasons. The Overlord stationed Vigot on Earth because his son had proven valuable in his prior battle positions and showed great intellect above his many brothers and sisters.

"Overlord, I know my journey, and I will walk the path. You need not travel all the way here just to warn me," Vigot brazenly responded to his father.

"Your journey is the same as my journey and the Overlords who have walked before me. We are the protectors of realms. We must maintain the balance, allowing no species to stand above us!" The Overlord crossed his arms, anger in his voice. "We are immortals, but we are not invincible. The human species is very unpredictable and volatile. You must keep them in their place, Vigot."

"I am a man, Overlord. I will do what is needed. I do not need a lecture," Vigot shouted back, his anger still apparent.

"You are a *young* man! Young men tend to think with their balls instead of their heads. Stay the course before you lose them both!" The Overlord roared through the tether, despite standing right in front of Vigot. A sharp pain ripped through Vigot's mind as his father sent one last warning shot. His father disappeared from the room, leaving Vigot on his knees, panting in pain.

Despite his father's brutal punishments, the Overlord had protected the demigods for centuries. Vigot had no right to question his father's commands or his tactics. Vigot was a young demigod, and many questioned the Overlord's decision to allow him to oversee their vital operations on Earth. He was the Overlord's youngest son, and his brothers openly disagreed with placing so much responsibility in the hands of someone so young. But Vigot had won many battles in his youth, some that even his older brothers couldn't have won. It was his father's guidance that made him strong. Vigot respected his father and would do anything commanded of him.

It also helped that Vigot's mother had the Overlord's ear when she suggested he give Vigot the position on Earth. Vigot's mother was a gorgeous ancient being who stoked fear in many. She was also a political powerhouse among the demigods. When she wanted something, she always found a way. She also had a keen sense of destiny. Despite everything Vigot had learned about their secret base on Earth, he still didn't know why his mother wanted him there. Before Vigot left his home world, his mother told him he would have to walk a path different from his father's. Vigot thought about his mother's warning.

Why send me to Earth if she knew I was destined to disobey my father, the Overlord?

~

The morning after their fall harvest festival, Tiago walked into breakfast with a massive chip on his shoulder. His curly black hair was tangled, and it looked like he didn't get much sleep. Everyone kept out of his way, especially Nhari and Kasha. But he wasn't going to let them off the hook that easily.

"Nhari, you betrayed me last night!" Tiago's face looked strained as he eyed Nhari directly. His azure eyes captured her attention, making it impossible for her to look away.

But Nhari didn't want to look away as tears rose in her eyes. She had never hurt Tiago before, and she could hear the pain in his voice.

Tiago looked at Kasha next. "You betrayed me too, Kasha. We were having a great fall harvest festival. Yet, the two of you were scheming behind my back the entire time!" He was rough in his assessment, and he seemed angrier the more he looked at them. He continued to stare and shout at them.

"What would have happened if the elemental children had lost their three protectors? Vigot could have killed all three of us. And way out there on the plains, no one would have discovered our bodies! We almost lost everything!" Tiago shouted.

"But Tiago, we didn't lose anything. Vigot didn't harm

me. He didn't harm any of us." Nhari tried to reason with him.

"We did lose something, Nhari. We lost our trust. Without trust, we are not a family. Without trust, we have lost the battle before it's begun. The demigods are our *captors!* They wield the sword that keeps us on our *knees!* They work for the ruling Guardian Clans, who cast prisoners here to die. The Guardian Clans, your own family, cast *you* out as a child, Nhari. You of all people should know the demigods can't be trusted." Tiago walked to the doorway and looked back once.

"Trust is everything. And if I don't have your trust, I don't want to be in this family anymore." Tiago left, the echoes of his footsteps a sad melody in the once lively cavern.

Kasha tried to follow him out, apologizing for keeping Nhari's secret. But Tiago wouldn't hear it. He knew he was hard on them, but they had to stay far away from the demigods. Kasha had been in the realm of the exiled her entire life and should have known better. She shouldn't have kept Nhari's dangerous secret. He couldn't have the two of them scheming behind his back. Tiago was the eldest and the most powerful of the elemental children. He had the final say. They had to respect him, or he was nothing. Tiago would not tolerate disrespect.

Kasha reentered the room crying, but she didn't look Nhari's way. Kasha went to her quarters without another word on the subject. She was also angry with Nhari. She told Nhari not to go on her date with Vigot, and she regretted helping her.

Nhari cried in anguish, lying on her bed as she thought about her actions.

What have I done? Maybe Tiago and Kasha are right. I was

part of the ruling Guardian Clan, a child of one of the most powerful leaders. But my family cast me out to die without a second thought. I was the youngest to ever be exiled, and I'm sure they all think I'm dead. In fact, they wanted me dead. And I would be dead if Tiago and Kasha didn't save me when I arrived in the realm of the exiled.

She wiped her eyes, looking around the home they had given her. *I betrayed the only true family I've ever had—my elemental family. I have to make this up to Tiago and win back his trust. I won't see Vigot again. I'll stay far away from him.*

An hour passed as Nhari tried to figure out what to do. She apologized to Kasha. Kasha forgave her, and the two hugged. As youthful beauties who were as close as sisters, they schemed up a plan to win Tiago over. But they knew it would take more than just the two of them to pull it off. They needed the help of all the elemental children.

When Tiago returned that evening, they had a surprise waiting for him. Tiago was met with part two of the fall harvest festival. But this time, it was a celebration of Tiago and all he meant to them. He was their leader, and they loved him dearly. Tiago forgave them.

Tiago, Kasha, Nhari and the elemental children partied and sang. They had a lavish meal of assorted spicy meats, cheeses, and desserts that Nhari labored all day to make. Kasha sang for everyone, her voice a beautiful mix of jazz and opera that pulled at their souls. They didn't have much, and they fought for everything they had in a prison never meant for children.

At the end of the night, they all held hands and made the sign of Suncorea. One by one, their elemental tattoos sprang to life, beautiful glyphs rotated from their joined hands to the ceiling above. Even those who hadn't reached puberty to develop their powers joined hands with the others. They didn't have elemental tattoos yet, but their energy still flowed. Black light was the brightest and most beautiful light in the universe. The elementals combined their power to create a stunning black light that streamed around the cavern, making an elaborate Suncorea sign before their eyes.

Together, the elementals were formidable and getting stronger each year. Tiago, Kasha, and Nhari continued to explore their growing elemental powers. Their elemental tattoos formed shimmering glyphs of elaborate and complex symbols. With love and steadfast determination, they protected the elemental children from the perils they faced living in the realm of the exiled.

For three years, the elemental children celebrated their fall harvest festival. Each festival was more glorious than the last. But things were about to change.

As Nhari sauntered down the corridors of the Braven on her twentieth birthday, the old fortune teller grabbed her hand and then hurried away. Nhari opened her hand, finding a strange note.

It read, "You will not see the next fall harvest festival in the realm of the exiled. But worry not, child. Good things are in store for the future of elementals."

EXILED NO MORE (EXILED ELEMENTALS) BOOK ONE

The youngest ever exiled, they believed it was a death sentence. But they were wrong. Nhari Evans survived brutal conditions living under the demigods' rule in prison. Ancient laws allowed her to return to civilization to battle for a seat on the guardian council that exiled her. Her family will stop at nothing to see her dead.

But Nhari has more than revenge pushing her to fight the strongest genetically engineered humans and demigods in a world where the environment is just as dangerous as her opponents. She has discovered her magical elemental powers and found others of her kind.

But like any young adult with too much power, mischief is addictive and dangerous lovers are drawn to her. Evil is spreading, and a balance must be restored.

Which side will she choose?

Find out in **EXILED NO MORE (Exiled Elementals Series) Book One**

ACKNOWLEDGMENTS

THANKS to the numerous people who helped make this book series an international success! My husband and three sons are my biggest fans. I appreciate all the times you listened to me talk about my journey into publication, enjoyed hearing what I had planned for my characters, and gave me the freedom to write no matter the time of day or night. I thank my mom, sisters, niece, and other family members who told the world about my story, held launch parties, and read every word of my books. You made my writing journey fun and memorable.

Thanks to my friends, social media followers, reviewers, and fellow authors for creating a buzz about the *Exiled Elementals Series*. I learned a lot from your questions, comments, and fun posts and pictures. Thanks to my beta readers, editors, publishing company, cover artists, and cartographers for providing creative touches that made the story come alive.

Thanks to the many readers and fans around the world who journeyed to the future to find out what would happen next to the cast of characters in the *Exiled Elementals Series*. I hope you find magic as you turn each page!

ABOUT THE AUTHOR

T. L. PRICE enjoys writing epic urban fantasy and paranormal romance novels with memorable characters full of intrigue, danger, and adventure. Come meet magical elementals, demigods, bioengineered humans, shifters, and others.

She writes fast-paced action scenes full of danger and steamy romance. Her exotic characters are strong-willed and unpredictable. Readers often cheer for more than one heroine or hero whose inspirational missions might be at odds in a dystopian world. She blends serious concepts with young adult characters and situations you can relate to. Her books make you think about destiny and the future while having you sitting on the edge of your seat, turning page after page for more.

When she's not running after her three sons in the Washington, D.C. area, enjoying dinner with her husband, or chatting with her sisters, she's writing amazing stories for you. The Realm of the Exiled is the prequel to the Exiled Elementals Series, which begins with Exiled No More, followed by Enviro-Scapes and Ruins Awakened.